The Long Journey

Balboa Press books may be ordered through booksellers or by contacting:

Balboa Press
A Division of Hay House
1663 Liberty Drive
Bloomington, IN 47403
www.balboapress.com
1 (877) 407-4847

ISBN: 978-1-9822-5072-0 (sc)
978-1-9822-5073-7 (e)

Library of Congress Control Number: 2020912453

Print information available on the last page.

Balboa Press rev. date: 07/21/2020

BALBOA.PRESS
A DIVISION OF HAY HOUSE

The Long Journey

A Tale of Friendship

Jeannine Pickering

In a state there was a city, and in that city there was a park.

In the park there was a bench, and under the bench there was an ant. The ant's name was Freddy and he was very scared.

Freddy wanted to get to the picnic table so he could get some food, but it was far and he did not want to get squished along the way.

Freddy began to cry.

A grasshopper heard the little ant's cry and went over to see if he could help. "What's wrong, little ant? You sound so sad!"

"I need help getting to the picnic table, but it is so far away!" Freddy said desperately.

"I'd be happy to help, but I only have time to take you to the big oak tree. Someone else will have to help you get to the picnic table from there."

Freddy happily agreed.

Freddy crawled onto the grasshopper's back and the grasshopper jumped and jumped until he got to the base of the big oak tree.

Freddy sat alone at the base of the tree and began to cry, yet again. A spider heard his cry and came to see what was going on.

"Hello little ant! Whatever could be wrong?"

"I need to get to the picnic table, but it is so far away, and I cannot get there by myself."

"I'd be happy to help, but only can get you to the large rock. You will have to find a way to the picnic table from there."

"Okay, that will do," Freddy said in desperation.

The spider carried Freddy on his back as he crawled to the large rock.

Freddy was so close to the picnic table, but he still could not get there by himself. Feeling hopeless, he began to cry yet again. A fluffy rabbit heard his cry and came over.

"What is wrong, little ant?"

"I need help getting to the picnic table, but everyone is too busy to take me there. If I go alone, I will get squished." Tears were running down Freddy's cheeks.

"I'm happy to help! I am on my way to the picnic table as well."

Freddy crawled onto the rabbit's back and the rabbit hopped to the table.

"Thank you, Mr. Rabbit! You are my hero!" Freddy squealed with joy.

"You are very welcome! It is my pleasure to help a friend in need."

Freddy had finally arrived at the picnic table and the food was plentiful. It was everything a hungry ant could wish for – Chocolate, watermelon, banana bread and juice. Suddenly, to Freddy's surprise, his other new friends showed up! Grasshopper and spider joined Freddy and Mr. Rabbit as they ate to their heart's content. Stuffed, the friends lay underneath the picnic table and drifted off to sleep. That day, Freddy and his friends had learned what a big impact one small gesture can have on someone's life.

Dedicated to our dog Smalls, always giving love to those that need it.

CPSIA information can be obtained
at www.ICGtesting.com
Printed in the USA
BVHW021428130920
588707BV00008B/299